HOW TO MAKE A FRIEND

by Stephen W. Martin

Illustrated by Olivia Aserr

Clarion Books
Houghton Mifflin Harcourt
Boston New York

For Lola—#include <iostream> int main()
{std::cout<<"MyBestfriend"<<std::endl; return 0;} —S.W.M.

To Jeremy and Bonnibel, my two best friends —O.A.

Clarion Books
3 Park Avenue
New York, New York 10016

Text copyright © 2021 by Stephen W. Martin
Illustrations copyright © 2021 by Olivia Aserr

Clarion Books is an imprint of Houghton Mifflin Harcourt Publishing Company.

hmhbooks.com

The text was set in Akkurat Pro.

Library of Congress Cataloging-in-Publication Data is available.
ISBN 978-1-328-63184-8

Manufactured in China
SCP 10 9 8 7 6 5 4 3 2 1
4500820711

Making a friend
can seem like a scary,
impossible task.
But trust me—

—with the right power tools and a basic understanding of Advanced Robotics, it's easy!

First things first:

Always, always wear safety goggles!

Next, you need to decide what kind of friend you want to make . . .

A friend to play with?

A friend to help you with homework?

A friend to crush your enemies?

Once you have chosen your friend, it's time to get to work.

Here are a few tips . . .

Measure twice,

cut once.

Ask your parents before handling plutonium.

And if you have any spare parts,
just hide them under your bed.

And there you have it! Your very own friend!

Now get out there—

and do all those awesome friend
things you've always wanted to do.

Tea parties,

hide-and-seek,

treehouse building,

and water fights!

Ah, wait . . . Water fights are not a good idea.

Now remember to share, take turns, and let your friend choose the game or activity sometimes.

Yes, having a best friend is pretty awesome!
You're probably finishing each other's sentences by now.

Don't be alarmed or upset if your friend
decides to make some other friends.

You don't have to play together all the time.

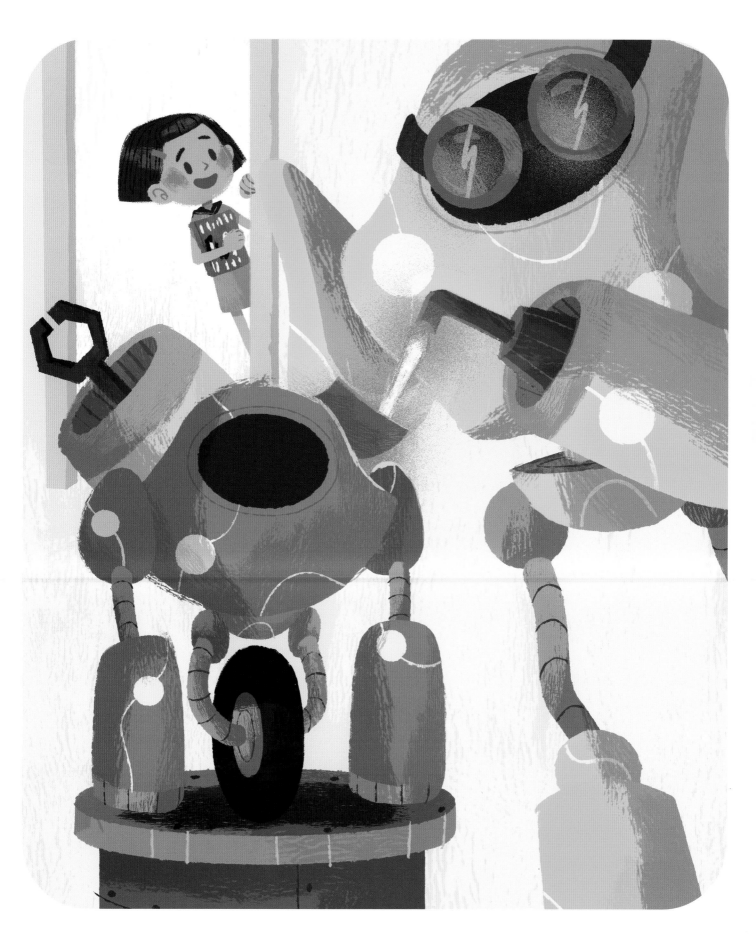

Plus, in time, they may even become your friends as well!

However, if you notice that your friend is hanging around with the wrong crowd or causing trouble, it's best to walk—

or in some cases *run* away!

If you're worried about them (or for the city),
make sure you tell a grownup.

And if things escalate . . .

well . . .

you planned for this.

Don't feel bad. Some
friendships just don't
work out . . .

for one reason or another.

It's not your fault (or ours . . . legally speaking).

Our advice is to take some time to reflect and recover,

especially if you were in the blast radius.

Then pick up the pieces—

really, anything you can salvage—

and start again.

We promise you that making a friend
will be 100% easier the second time.